W9-CZH-337

HOLDING THE
YELLOW RABBIT

by Bonnie Highsmith Taylor

For
Amber Jones, Ashley Jones, and Ryan Jones
Heather Austin and Shelby Miller
Krystal McCown
Megan Highsmith

B. T.

Cover Illustration: Doug Knutson
Inside Illustration: Larassa Kabel

About the Author

Bonnie Highsmith Taylor is a native Oregonian. She loves camping in the Oregon mountains and watching birds and other wildlife. Writing is Ms. Taylor's first love. But she also enjoys going to plays and concerts, collecting antique dolls, and listening to good music. The idea for *Holding the Yellow Rabbit* came when she picked up an old cardboard rabbit in an antique shop. She began to wonder about the child who may have received it for Easter a long, long time ago. The child turned out to be Jamie. *Holding the Yellow Rabbit* is his story.

Text © 1998 by Perfection Learning® Corporation.

All rights reserved. No part of this book may be used or reproduced in any manner whatsoever without written permission from the publisher.

Printed in the United States of America. For information, contact Perfection Learning® Corporation, 1000 North Second Avenue, P.O. Box 500, Logan, Iowa 51546-1099

Paperback 0-7891-2159-x

Cover Craft® 07-807-6784-5

9 10 PP 08 07 06 05

Contents

1. The Big News 5

2. The House 13

3. The Decision 20

4. The Yellow Rabbit. 24

5. The Picture 32

6. The First Night. 38

7. The Library 46

8. The Letter 55

9. The Lavaliere. 60

1

The Big News

Dad announced to the family at dinner that his company was opening a new office and he was to be the manager. At first, we were all excited.

"Well, it's about time," said Mom. "After all these years."

"Cool, Dad," I said. Vanessa and Susan loudly agreed.

"Will we be rich?" asked six-year-old Susan.

"Hardly," Dad laughed. "But we will be able to afford something we've always wanted."

"A new car?" I offered.

"There's nothing wrong with our old car, Jimmy," Dad explained, "except that it's not quite paid for yet."

"A computer?" Vanessa suggested. "Or a big-screen television? Or both!"

Dad shook his head.

"I know!" cried Susan. "A horse!" I groaned aloud at Susan's suggestion as I slouched back in the chair.

"Don't be silly," Vanessa said. "It wouldn't be a horse!"

"But Daddy said it was something we've always wanted. And a horse *is* something I've always wanted."

"Dad said something *all* of us have always wanted," said Vanessa. "Not just *you.*"

"So," replied Susan, sticking her nose in the air.

"Besides, you always want everything," Vanessa went on. "And you usually get it."

"Do not!" Susan pouted.

"Do too!" spat Vanessa.

"Do not!"

"Do too!"

"That's enough!" demanded Mom, and I silently agreed. Susan began eating her muffin, and Vanessa picked at her salad. Both girls were glaring at each other over their food. I began to giggle at them but quickly stopped as Mom looked my way.

Mom looked hopefully at Dad and asked, "John, are you by any chance talking about a house?"

Dad's grin told us that she'd guessed right. Mom gave a happy sigh and took a sip of tea.

The rest of us gave a happy yell.

"It'll be great to get out of this apartment and live in a house," Mom said. "I can hardly wait."

"A house with a big yard, I hope," I added. "Big enough to play baseball."

"And close to our school," Vanessa said. "It will be close to school, won't it?"

Dad cleared his throat and took a long drink of tea.

We all looked at Dad, but Dad wasn't looking at anyone. I had a bad feeling about the way he was acting.

After a brief, uncomfortable silence, he said, "Please pass the potatoes, Marsha."

Mom passed the potatoes and began to ask, "John—"

"Will you pass the butter please?" Dad interrupted.

Mom quickly passed the butter and began again, "John—"

Dad cut in again, "After dinner, okay? Then we'll talk about it, and I'll tell you all you want to know— and then some."

We all hurried through dinner. Then we went into the living room and waited for Dad to begin.

The first thing Dad shared was, "The job is in—in another town."

"Another town!" shrieked Vanessa as she jumped up from the couch. "You mean I'll have to change schools?"

I felt the same way that Vanessa did. I didn't want to move to another town. I'd have to leave all my friends. I'd gone to the same school all my life. And in the fall I'd be starting junior high.

Dad's good news didn't sound so good to me after all. Maybe living in an apartment wasn't that bad.

And I can always play baseball at the park or at the school playground, I thought. It isn't *that* far to walk.

Very slowly Mom asked, "What town, John?"

"Glenhaven," Dad answered, trying to make it sound exciting.

"Glenhaven," said Mom. "I've never heard of it."

"Well it's, oh, about a hundred miles from here," Dad explained.

"Oh, no!" whined Vanessa, flopping back down on the couch. But nobody paid any attention to her.

"Is a hundred miles a long way, Daddy?" questioned Susan.

"Well, it's not across the country," Dad assured her.

"It's only about a two-hour drive from here."

"But two hours is a long time, isn't it?" said Susan. And after she thought about it a bit more, she added, "I won't be able to sleep over at Becky's or Kim's anymore. I won't be able to go to story hour at the library. I'll have to stop my ballet—" By now Susan was whining too.

I even felt like whining. If I was little like Susan or even ten like Vanessa, I would have. But twelve-year-olds aren't supposed to whine. I knew I'd never get away with it, anyway.

No one said anything for a minute or two. Then Mom asked, "John, how big is Glenhaven?"

"Not—not big," Dad stammered.

"How big?" Mom insisted.

"Well—I guess it's what you'd call a—a small town," Dad replied carefully. "Actually, a very charming small town."

"Oh, no!" Vanessa started whining all over again, wallowing all over the couch.

Susan joined in on the whining and wallowing. "Oh, no! Not a small town!"

I poked Susan with my elbow. "Be quiet! You don't even know what you're talking about."

"Ouch! I do too!"

"Do not!"

"Do too!"

"Stop it, both of you!" ordered Mom. "John, I think it's wonderful about *your* new job, but what about *my* job? There's not much chance of finding anything in a small town."

Dad perked up and replied, "That's another thing I wanted to tell you, Marsha! You know how you've *always* said you'd like to have your own antique shop? Well, my boss said he's *sure* that Glenhaven doesn't have one!"

I looked over at Mom and saw her face instantly light up. "An antique shop," she said, her eyes glazing over. "Hmmm."

Well, Dad's won Mom over, I thought. All he has to do is convince Susan, Vanessa, and me that it will be nice to move away from our school and all of our friends. And how wonderful it will be to live in a town that probably isn't even on the map!

Dad wasn't finished yet. "Marsha," he said, "the way you like antiques, you might be interested in a house I heard about. My boss gave me the name of the real estate man who has the listing, and I called him."

Mom looked puzzled. "What in the world do antiques have to do with buying a house?" She paused and then continued with growing interest. "Unless it's an old run-down house that's a couple hundred years old. John?"

Dad said hurriedly, "It's not really run-down. And

it's only about 85 years old. That's not old for a house."

"Go on," prodded Mom.

Dad went on, "It's a real buy."

"Why?" Mom asked as she scooted to the edge of her chair. "Why is it a real buy?"

"Because—because it's been empty for a few years." I perked up a little, wondering what was wrong with it.

"I see," said Mom. She looked directly at Dad. "Why has it been empty for a few years?"

Dad attempted a laugh, which I decided didn't quite make it. "Well—" he gulped, "it seems that about 80 years ago, the family who lived there sort of—well, they just disappeared."

"Disappeared!" we all exclaimed. I couldn't believe it! And neither could my stomach, which suddenly acted as though it didn't want its dinner anymore.

"A robber broke in," Dad continued, "and—well— they never found out for sure what happened to the family. But from the way things looked, the family was—"

Mom gave Dad a "not in front of the kids" look. But Dad continued anyway.

"They may as well know, Marsha," said Dad. "Everyone in Glenhaven knows about it. That's why no one stays in the house for very long."

Vanessa let out a squeal. "I can't believe our own

father would ask us to move into a house where something so *awful* happened. It's probably *haunted*. It's probably full of *ghosts*. Why else would no one want to live in it?"

"It is not haunted," stated Dad. "Now, I told the real estate man we'd meet him at the house tomorrow afternoon, Marsha. Okay?"

I stared hard at Mom, trying to let her know my feelings through the horrified look on my face. But Mom made a face and then gave a big sigh. "Okay, we'll *just* take a look at it."

Oh, no!

2
The House

The next afternoon we drove to Glenhaven. Vanessa sat glumly, staring out the window the entire drive. Susan fell asleep. Her head kept bobbing over onto my shoulder. As soon as I pushed her away, it bobbed back. Finally, I gave up and let her lean on me.

I looked out the window at the passing countryside. I grew more interested in our venture as we passed a small lake and Dad said, "Maybe we can get a boat, Jimmy."

We turned left on Chestnut Lane. I could see an old, grayish house through the trees. It was set back from the road a bit. As we neared the house, I saw a man sitting on the front steps. A red car was parked in the driveway.

"That's Mr. Hill from the real estate office," Dad said.

Dad slowed down in front of the house and turned into the driveway. As we rolled to a stop, Susan finally looked up and asked, "Are we there yet?"

Vanessa muttered, "Whoop-dee-doo."

We climbed out of the car, stretched, and looked around. Dad shook hands with Mr. Hill.

The yard was huge! It was big enough for a baseball diamond. It was filled with lots of big, old trees.

Across the road was a big field and rolling hills beyond. The hills were covered with trees too. What a great place to go hiking! I'll be able to take wildlife and nature pictures with my new camera.

I knew then that I wanted more than anything to live there. I didn't care how small the town was. And I could always get used to a new school—in time.

I glanced over at Mom. The look on her face let me

know what she thought of the place so far.

I heard her say softly to Dad, "Oh, good heavens, John."

Dad took her arm and led her toward the house. "Let's at least look at the inside," he said quietly. "It might not be too bad."

Oh, please don't let her say no, I thought. I loved it already—even without seeing the inside.

"It's spooky," said Susan. "I don't like it here."

"But look at all those big trees," I said.

I grabbed Susan's hand and pulled her along through the tall grass and weeds. We stepped over broken limbs on the ground. Susan groaned softly, still groggy after her nap. "It's spooky," she repeated.

"But after the grass is cut and it's cleaned up, it will be nice," I said. "Maybe Dad and I will put up a swing for you on one of those high branches. Maybe we can make a tree house. Wouldn't you like that?"

Susan's eyes brightened a little, but she still held back.

I squeezed her hand. "Come on, let's see what it's like inside. It must have an upstairs. There's a window over the front porch."

At least it looked like a window. It was so dark and grimy it was hard to tell.

Mr. Hill unlocked the front door, and we all followed him inside.

The house wasn't as big as I had thought it would be. But it was nice. Even though everything was covered with cobwebs and several inches of dust.

The windows were so dirty you couldn't see through them. Out of the corner of my eye, I saw Mom wince as she looked around the room.

There was a big stone fireplace at one end of the living room.

"See, Susan," I said. "A fireplace to hang your stocking at Christmas. You've never done that before."

Susan's hand relaxed a little in mine.

"And a chimney for Santa to come down," I continued. "We can have roaring fires in the winter and roast marshmallows."

Susan smiled.

Pulling her hand, I followed everyone down the hallway, brushing away cobwebs.

Mr. Hill was saying, "It's a charming old house. Professor Harriman had it built when he first came to Glenhaven. He was the director of the museum in Weston, which is about ten miles from here."

"How many were in the Harriman family?" Mom asked.

Mr. Hill said, "The professor and his wife and their nine-year-old son."

I gasped. Nine years old! Just a little kid! How could anyone do such a thing? Especially to a child!

Mr. Hill opened the first door off the hall. "This is the master bedroom," he said. "It's quite large. Notice the nice hardwood floors."

Dad agreed that the floors were nice and the house was certainly well-built. But Mom still had a look of disappointment on her face.

"Oh, please," I kept praying. "Don't say no."

Vanessa stuck her head inside the open closet. She drew back hurriedly. "Oh, yuck!" she cried, wiping cobwebs from her face.

"Oh, yuck!" echoed Susan.

We walked down the hall and past the bathroom.

"This is the other bedroom," Mr. Hill said.

"*Other* bedroom?" I repeated. "You mean there are only *two* bedrooms?"

"That settles it," Mom said with a big sigh of relief. "We need three bedrooms. The children certainly can't all share one room."

Dad looked very disappointed.

"There is a small room upstairs," the real estate man said. "It's only an attic, but with a little work it would make a fine room for someone." He smiled at me and said, "Especially if that someone liked privacy."

We climbed the steep stairway to the little room over the front part of the house. It was almost totally dark. The window was completely covered with cobwebs.

The room smelled musty. And the floor creaked as we walked across it.

Mr. Hill pulled the chain that hung from the light fixture on the ceiling. He had to jiggle it before it would turn on.

Mom looked more disgusted than ever.

Vanessa was holding her nose with one hand and covering her mouth with the other.

Susan sneezed. Then I sneezed. Then Dad sneezed.

Dust was everywhere.

"You certainly don't expect one of our children to sleep in this mess," Mom said to Dad, in a very angry voice. She didn't even seem to care that a stranger was listening.

I had to agree with Mom—in a way. It was pretty awful!

But that big yard with all those trees. The fireplace. The field across the road. The lake close by...

I looked around the small, filthy room. I went to the window and tried to look out. I picked up an old cloth that was lying on the floor and wiped at the grime-covered glass. Through the round spot, I could see the hills in the distance. Beyond the hills were snow-capped mountains. Just past the old picket fence at the edge of the yard was a thicket of blackberries.

I thought of my bedroom at home. It was no bigger than this room. And from my window, I could see only the brick wall of the next building. In the summer it was hot and stuffy. And the traffic noise was terrible!

"I wouldn't mind sleeping in this room, Mom," I said. "Honest I wouldn't. Dad and I could fix it up. We could—"

Mom interrupted with, "We'll discuss it later."

While Mom went through the kitchen opening cupboards and storage closets, I wandered around the rest of the house. I wondered if the back bedroom had been the little boy's. I wondered if he'd hung his stocking over the fireplace on Christmas Eve. I wondered if the trees had been here then. Did the boy climb them? Did he have a tree house? Did he play in that field across the road?

Poor little kid. I shuddered and went outside.

A short time later, Mr. Hill left. He asked Dad to call him when we had reached a decision.

Dad walked beside Mom as they went to the car. "What do you think, Marsha? It's a great buy. As creative as you are with decorating, you could have it looking beautiful in a few months."

I held my breath, waiting for Mom's answer.

But again she said, "We'll discuss it later."

3
The Decision

Mom and Dad did discuss the house on the way home. But it seemed to me that Mom was doing most of the discussing. Dad and I couldn't get a word in.

Vanessa, of course, was agreeing with Mom. "It is pretty gross, Dad."

Susan couldn't make up her mind. She liked the nice yard, but not the ghosts. "I don't want to live in a house that has spooky old ghosts running around," she said.

"Oh, Susan," Dad reasoned. "There are no such things as ghosts. They're only in stories."

"But they could get *out* of stories," Susan explained. "They could get *in* that house. It's haunted. Vanessa said so."

"You know better than that, Vanessa," Dad said. "You're ten years old. Much too old to believe in things like that." Vanessa slumped back in the seat with a scowl on her face.

"Ghosts or no ghosts," Mom said, "the place is a dump. No wonder no one will live in it."

"But, Marsha," Dad said, "it can be cleaned up. We can paint and put down carpets. We can have it rewired. Maybe we can add new siding and a new roof."

"The reason people won't live there is because of what happened a long time ago," I joined in. "It's *not* because the house is run-down and dirty."

"That's another thing I don't like about it," Mom answered. "To live in a house where people were— were—" She looked at Dad and continued. "How can you even think of living where something so horrible took place?"

"But it happened 80 years ago," Dad reminded her.

Mom was speechless, but Vanessa wasn't. "What difference does it make to a ghost how long it's been dead?"

Dad smacked himself on the forehead. He moaned, "I give up. If you want me to give up the chance of a lifetime. If you want to go on living in a stuffy apartment instead of owning our own home, it's fine with me. Let's just forget it."

We rode along in complete silence. I felt kind of sorry for Dad. I knew that he really wanted this job.

After a while, Mom gave a big sigh and said, "Well, I guess it would look better after a good scrubbing. And after some paint and wallpaper." She grinned back at Vanessa, who had her face screwed up something awful. "And if there are any ghosts in that house, we'll give them brooms and dust cloths and make them help us."

"Cool!" I yelled.

"Cool!" shouted Susan.

"Oooh!" groaned Vanessa.

"I'll call Mr. Hill in the morning and let him know we're taking it," said Dad. "I can't believe we're getting such a great deal!"

Vanessa started to speak, but Dad interrupted her. "And it's not because the house is haunted."

Mom reached back and patted Vanessa. "It'll be all right, honey," she said. "Soon it'll be cleaned and painted. We'll get our belongings all in place, and you won't even remember what it looked like. And Daddy will have a good job."

She sure changed her mind in a hurry, I thought. Now if Vanessa would just change hers. Susan didn't seem to mind one way or another.

"And another thing," Mom informed us. "Mr. Hill said the desk and a few other pieces are to go with the house. They're antiques, you know."

Holy cow! Did Mom change her mind because of that old junk? I knew that she was big on antiques, but…. Oh, well. She changed her mind, and that was all that mattered.

When we got back to town, we celebrated at The Pizza Palace.

Dad was in a great mood. He even stopped by the ice cream parlor and got cones for everyone.

That night, I couldn't get to sleep. We were actually going to live in a house. A house with a big yard! And hills and lakes!

I grinned in the dark. And maybe a ghost or two.

What if there really were such things as ghosts? I thought. What if the ghost of the little boy lived in the old house? It sure was sad thinking about a ghost who was just a kid.

Another thought crossed my mind. If the little boy were alive today, he would be almost 90 years old. He would be an old, old man!

4
The Yellow Rabbit

Saturday morning we went back to the house in Glenhaven. We took along enough cleaning products and disinfectants to clean the Empire State Building!

When we pulled into the driveway, a rabbit ran out of the tall grass. He ran through the yard and disappeared around an old shed.

"Ooh!" cried Susan. "Will you catch it for me, Daddy? I want it for a pet."

Dad laughed. "You don't make pets out of wild animals, Susan. Besides, you'll probably see it again. You'll most likely see other wild animals too. Mr. Hill said he even saw a fox in that field across the road."

Vanessa gave a great sigh and remarked, "Oh, great! It's not enough that we're moving into a haunted house. Now we have to worry about being killed by foxes!"

"Good heavens, Vanessa!" Dad roared. "Foxes don't kill people."

"Even I knew that," said Mom.

I couldn't keep from laughing. Vanessa was such a scaredy-cat!

It was time to get some cleaning done. Dad had borrowed a lawnmower and rake from Uncle George. He went right to work on the big lawn.

Mom said, "Susan, you can help Daddy put the grass in the trash bags. Vanessa, you'll help me scrub the kitchen cupboards and walls."

She handed me a box and said, "You go upstairs and pick up all that junk lying around."

I carried the empty box through the house and up the stairs to the attic. Looking around, I could see that my work was cut out for me. I opened the window in the attic to let in some fresh air. It was all I could do to pry it loose.

The fresh air felt good. I could smell the roses that were climbing an old trellis by the front porch. I scanned the meadow across the road, hoping to see a deer or a fox. I saw lots of birds. "Maybe Dad will help me build some birdhouses and a feeder," I thought.

After viewing the scenery, I decided that the big cleaning job would certainly be worth it. I brushed down cobwebs with a whisk broom and shook them out the window. I'd never seen so much dust and cobwebs in my life!

I sneezed a lot because of the dust. Luckily, I'd worn really old clothes. I was covered with dust and filth in no time!

I began to put some of the junk in the box Mom had given me. There were old newspapers, a couple of milk bottles—Mom would love those—and a mousetrap. I was sure glad to find that empty.

There were walnuts rolling around on the floor. Some small animals must have stashed them away. It was probably squirrels. Surely with all those trees there would be some squirrels.

I picked up what I thought was an old hatbox. I started to drop it in with the other trash, but stopped. I noticed a metal clasp on it and said aloud, "This looks like some kind of case." I shook it and noticed that something was inside.

The latch was rusted shut. I looked around and found a stick. I used the stick to pry the box open.

Wow! The old box was full of toys! These must have belonged to the boy who lived here. I sat down on the floor and took everything out of the case, one by one. There were 12 lead soldiers, a bag of marbles, a spinning top, a little wooden boat, some chalk, and a ball and jacks.

I lined the lead soldiers up on the floor. As I did, I felt a chill go through my body. Just a breeze from the window, I thought.

I was excited about finding the toys. But I sure felt strange handling the belongings of someone who had died.

I thought of the little boy playing with these very toys. Maybe he even sat in this very spot!

I began to wonder if the boy would care if I played with his toys. Maybe he'd want someone to have his things. He might want someone to take care of them.

When Mom called everyone for lunch, I took the case and the milk bottles down. Mom put the bottles in the sink to soak.

I opened the case and said, "See what I found?"

"The little boy's toys!" Mom gasped. "How sad."

Dad picked up the top. "I remember my grandfather telling about spinning these tops when he was a boy. There's quite a talent to it."

He unwound the string around the top. It crumbled into several pieces.

Susan took the rubber ball out of the box. She tried to bounce it on the floor, but it landed with a thud.

"I wouldn't touch those things for anything in the world," said Vanessa.

"Why not?" I asked, annoyed that she was such a scaredy-cat.

"I wouldn't want to get some ghost mad at me. Even if it is just a little kid," she shot back at me.

"Aw, come on. That's dumb," I said, trying to convince her. I guess I should've chosen my words more carefully, though.

"You think so?" Vanessa replied. "Well, how would you like it if you were dead? And then some kid you didn't even know came along and played with your toys?"

"I wouldn't care," I answered. She was acting so silly. "Besides, I'm not playing with them."

"That's enough, now," Mom said. "I've had enough of this arguing."

"I can keep these things, can't I?" I asked, looking hopefully at Mom and Dad.

"I don't know why not," said Dad.

"But take good care of them, dear," Mom said. "They're antiques, you know. They're worth a lot of money."

"My gosh, Mom," I said, but not very loud.

As we ate, I noticed the cleaning that Mom and Vanessa had done. I thought the kitchen was starting to look pretty good. The cupboards, which looked gray, turned out to be almost white.

After lunch, we all went back to our chores. I headed back upstairs with the box of toys.

In the attic, I took the toys out and looked at them again. Toys were sure a lot different back then. I picked up the wooden boat and turned it over in my hands.

That little boy would be an old, old man if he were still alive. This little attic room might have been his favorite place to play. Now it was my place.

I set the toys aside and got back to work. As I swept down more cobwebs, I thought about what Vanessa had said. Would the little Harriman boy really be mad if he knew I was playing with his toys?

"I'll take good care of them. Honest I will."

I realized then that I had spoken out loud. I felt a little silly. I even glanced at the stairway. I sure didn't want anyone to hear me talking to myself!

I'd better get this stuff cleaned up, especially before Mom comes up, I decided.

I scrunched up a stack of papers in my arms and pushed them down into the box. As I pushed down with the flat of my hand, I felt a lump in the newspapers. I figured that one of the papers must've gotten wadded up.

I reached into the middle of the pile. To my surprise, I pulled something out, and it wasn't newspaper! I walked over to the window and held it in the light.

"A rabbit!" I exclaimed aloud. "A cardboard rabbit!"

I'd seen them in Mom's antique books. They were made out of hard, rough cardboard. Kids used to get them for Easter.

I blew the dust off the rabbit. It was yellow. It was pretty faded, but it was yellow. It had a painted blue bow around its neck.

I held it in my hands carefully and stared at it.

Suddenly, I felt someone in the room with me. Funny, I hadn't even heard anyone come up the stairs. It's probably just Vanessa nosing around.

"What do you want?" I said, annoyed. "Go downstairs. I'm busy."

I looked up, expecting to see Vanessa. But it wasn't Vanessa. It wasn't anyone. I was all alone in the room.

I sure felt funny. I shook my head hard. Something seemed to have touched me. But what?

My hand holding the rabbit felt sweaty. I felt my skin crawl.

I looked all around the room. "I could have sworn someone, or something, was standing next to me," I whispered. "And why do I feel so strange?"

On wobbly legs, I walked over to the case of toys on the floor. I placed the yellow rabbit on the top.

Just like that, whatever I had felt was gone.

I put my head out the window and inhaled deeply. It's pretty stuffy up here, I thought. That must be it. I just got overheated.

I decided I'd probably worked enough for one day. I carried the box of junk downstairs and dumped it into a plastic bag.

5
The Picture

The next day, we went back to our new house for more cleaning. Vanessa, of course, grumbled and complained the whole way. Susan said she was too tired to help. She perked right up, though, when Dad mentioned raking up the old leaves and jumping in them.

I couldn't wait to get there. Throughout the drive, I thought about what had happened the day before.

"We haven't even made a dent in all this dirt and grime," Mom announced to everyone as we filed into the kitchen. "The sooner we get this place in shape, the sooner we can move in. So let's get at it."

"Aye, aye," said Dad as he saluted.

Mom laughed and popped him with a cleaning rag.

"Vanessa and I will start on the master bedroom," Mom went on. "And Susan, you can help Daddy clean the yard some more."

To me she said, "You finish cleaning upstairs. Then take one of these rags and the furniture oil. You can work on that old desk and bookcase in the living room."

My legs trembled as I climbed the stairs. I still couldn't stop thinking about that strange feeling I'd had yesterday. The feeling that someone was in the room with me. I remembered that I had been holding the yellow rabbit at the time.

I've never felt that way in my life! It was weird— really weird. I hope I'm not getting as silly as Vanessa, I thought to myself.

The sun was shining through the window this morning. So the room didn't seem as dismal as it had before.

This room won't be so bad, I thought. Especially when Dad gets it sealed in and we paint it. And, like Mr. Hill had said, I'll have privacy. I can play my stereo as loud as I want.

I remembered that Mom told me we'd put tile on the floor. She said I could even pick it out.

"I'll have my bed right under the window," I said aloud. "So I can look out and see the hills first thing every morning. And my desk will go on that wall." I pictured it in my mind. I thought I'd even ask Mom if I could have a chair over in the corner.

I walked over to the corner so I could see just how a chair would fit. The corner where I'd put the case of toys the day before. And where I'd put the yellow rabbit.

But—but there *was* no rabbit in the corner! The case was there, but the rabbit was gone!

I felt the air leave my lungs. No one else had been in this room. No one. And I had put the rabbit on the case. I was sure of it.

My eyes darted around the room. Then I spied it. The yellow rabbit was on the floor under the window. It couldn't have just fallen off the case. The window was at least eight feet away!

I picked up the rabbit and held it in my hands. That strange feeling came back. The feeling that someone was there. I felt goose pimples breaking out all over.

"Who are you?" I whispered.

I was sure something brushed my arm. But no one was there. Then, something brushed me again!

"Are you the boy who used to live here?" I asked aloud to the empty room.

What was I saying? I'm as bad as Vanessa. It was crazy—absolutely crazy!

"There are no such things as ghosts!" I yelled. I wanted out of there. I set the rabbit down and ran out the door and down the stairs. At the bottom, I stopped a minute to catch my breath and slow my beating heart.

"Are you already finished?" Mom called from the bedroom.

"No, Mom," I answered, panting. "I—I thought I'd oil the bookshelves and desk first. I'll finish upstairs later."

My heart was still thumping like crazy. Calm down, I told myself. If they notice that I'm afraid, they'll think I'm weird too. They might even decide not to move in if they think *all* their kids are going batty, I worried.

I rubbed the oiled cloth hard over each shelf of the bookcase in the living room. My mind raced wildly. Something about that yellow rabbit was eerie. What was it that made me feel so strange when I held it in my hands?

It was like—like—I didn't know what. I couldn't explain it. I'd never had such a feeling. Except maybe when I woke up after having a bad dream.

But this was no dream. This was real. And yet—

The rabbit must have fallen off the case. It must have fallen hard and bounced to where I'd found it.

There was no other way it could have happened. No other way.

I was still trying to reason with myself when Susan came into the room. "What are you doing?" she asked.

"Dusting and oiling this old stuff for Mom," I answered. I was glad to have someone around.

"Can I help?"

"Sure. You can open the drawers on that old desk. Then I can clean the cobwebs and dust out."

"Ooo!" Susan squealed, as she pulled open a drawer. "A spider! A giant spider!"

I scooped the spider onto a magazine. It wasn't even close to being a giant. I carried it outside and shook it off the magazine and into the grass.

"It's bad luck to kill a spider," I said when Susan asked why I didn't squash it.

Carefully, Susan pulled at another drawer. "This one is stuck," she said. "Help me."

I tried it. It was stuck fast. I gave the drawer a jerk, and it came out, nearly knocking me on the floor.

Something landed beside me.

"A picture!" Susan exclaimed. "A picture of a little boy!"

I picked it up.

"It must have been stuck in the drawer," I said, studying the boy in the photograph. He had curly hair and he was smiling. He was wearing a sailor suit with short pants.

I turned the picture over. On the back was written: *Jamie—Easter, 1916.*

Jamie.

I smiled. The boy's name was Jamie. It was probably really James, the same as mine.

"What's he holding in his hand?" Susan asked when I turned the picture over again.

"A rabbit, Susan. A yellow rabbit."

Susan put her face close to the picture. "But the picture isn't colored. How do you know the rabbit is yellow?"

"I just know," I answered.

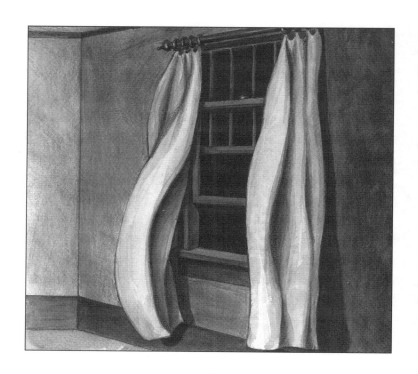

6

The First Night

Two weeks later, the house was finally clean and ready for us. We'd worked hard. Now it was actually livable!

Dad rented a moving van, and we had to make three trips. I was surprised we had that much stuff.

Earlier in the week, Dad had suggested having a garage sale. "We can get rid of this old junk."

"I'll have you know," Mom replied, "that I don't own any *junk*. Just because something is old doesn't make it junk."

I was beginning to agree with Mom about old things. I thought about the yellow rabbit and the other toys.

I was even glad that the house was old. Mom was right when she said that its age gave it character.

Vanessa had cried the whole time she was packing her things. "Here's the music box my best friend Holly gave me on my birthday," she sniffled. "I'll never see her again."

Mom tried to make her feel better. "We're not moving that far away, Vanessa. You can call her once in a while. And maybe she can come for visits next summer."

"It's just not the same," replied Vanessa.

I knew how Vanessa felt. I'd had a hard time saying good-bye to my friends too. Kids I'd gone to school with since kindergarten. I'd felt sad when I saw my school for the last time.

But that feeling didn't last long. Now I was looking forward to moving into our new home.

Dad hadn't finished the attic room yet. I'd have to sleep on the couch for a few nights.

The rest of the house looked great. Every room had been painted. The bedrooms and living room had been carpeted.

Vanessa was even pleased with the room she'd be sharing with Susan. She almost stopped complaining about moving.

If only she knew, I thought.

When we finally finished unpacking, we were starving. We were all excited to eat our first dinner in the new house.

When we were done with dinner, I went upstairs to my room. I took the yellow rabbit out of the case and held it. The feeling of someone standing next to me was so real that I reached out my hand.

Why couldn't I touch him? He was there. I knew he was. But you can't touch a ghost—can you?

I took a deep breath. "J—Jamie," I whispered. "I'm Jimmy. James Nolan." My voice trembled. "I like your rabbit a lot. I hope you don't mind if I keep it."

A wave of cool air touched my face. It was a soft, feathery breeze.

I smiled. "Thanks, Jamie. Thank you."

———

Later in the evening, Mr. Hill dropped in to see how we were coming along.

"I can't believe this is the same place," he said. "You've done wonders with it."

Mom and Dad beamed as they showed him around. Throughout his tour, Mr. Hill spoke glowingly about the changes and all the hard work we'd done.

"I'm sure you're going to be happy here," he said. "You've put a lot of tender loving care into it. This must have been a very fine home when the professor and his family lived here."

"It's such a shame," Mom said sadly, "the terrible thing that happened."

"Yes," Mr. Hill agreed. "I still think that if they hadn't put the story about the lavaliere in the paper—"

"Lavaliere," said Dad. "What about a lavaliere?"

"What's that?" asked Susan.

I was glad Susan asked. I sure didn't know what it was. I didn't think from the look on Vanessa's face that she knew either.

Mom explained, "A lavaliere is a lovely necklace with a pendant."

Mr. Hill said, "Professor Harriman was an archeologist. He had just returned from a dig at an Indian burial ground. He'd found a silver lavaliere. But it wasn't Indian. It was Spanish. Beautiful Spanish silver, they say. The professor believed that it may have been traded to the Wichita Indians by Coronado or his men. They explored the region in 1541."

I drew in my breath.

"It was said to be worth as much as $50,000. That was a lot of money back in 1917."

That's a lot of money anytime! I thought.

"Professor Harriman hired a young man to do some work around the museum. People believed he was responsible for the crime," said Mr. Hill. "He was after the silver lavaliere."

"Did they ever catch him?" asked Dad.

"Not exactly," said Mr. Hill. "The young man sailed on a ship to South America the next day. There was a terrible storm at sea. The ship went down, and he was drowned."

"Good," said Vanessa. "I'm glad he didn't get away with it."

"But the lavaliere went with him," said Mr. Hill. "The professor had the lavaliere at his home over the weekend. He planned to take it to the museum on Monday. The police think the Harrimans were murdered on Sunday evening."

I tried to swallow the lump in my throat. I was sure glad when Mr. Hill left. I didn't like hearing about the horrible thing that had happened in our house.

That evening, Dad built a big fire in the fireplace. It was so warm we had to open all the windows and doors. Then we roasted marshmallows. It was the most fun we'd had together in a long time.

Before long, it was bedtime. We were all worn out from the move. Finally, everyone was in bed, and all the lights were out. It was sure strange sleeping in a new house.

I lay on the couch in the dark room and thought about Jamie. I wondered exactly how he had died. But, no! I decided not to think about it. It gave me the creeps!

I wondered what it was like being a boy back then. There wouldn't have been television. And they only had silent movies.

Jamie would have been alive when the Boston Red Sox won the World Series three years in a row. Babe Ruth was the pitcher. I wondered if Jamie liked baseball the way I did. If Jamie had lived, he might have watched my all-time favorite player—Hank Aaron.

If only Jamie could talk to me. It would be almost like having a little brother. A little brother who's a ghost.

"Cool," I whispered aloud in the dark.

Suddenly, a loud crash followed by a high-pitched scream brought me to my feet.

It has to be Vanessa, I thought. No one else screams like that!

Dad and Mom were right behind me when I reached the girls' room. Mom switched on the light. Vanessa was huddled against the wall in her bed, screaming her lungs out.

Susan, half-asleep, was sobbing, "Mama, Mama."

Dad grabbed Vanessa up in his arms. "What's wrong, Vanessa? Tell us what's wrong!"

I thought for sure her eyes were going to pop right

out of her head. Her arms were wrapped around Dad's neck so tight that he started choking.

"Vanessa, dear," Mom said. "What is it?"

"A—a ghost," Vanessa panted. "I knew this house was haunted."

"Oh, Vanessa," Dad gurgled, pulling her arms from around his neck. "You must have had a bad dream."

I looked around the room. "Look!" I cried.

The lamp that had been on the nightstand was now on the floor.

Mom picked it up. "John," she said almost in a whisper, "how could this have happened?"

Just then a gust of wind came through the open window. It blew the curtain up.

"That's how it happened," Dad said. "The wind blew it over."

"N—No," Vanessa cried. "It—it was a ghost. I know it was a ghost."

Susan started crying harder than ever. "I want to sleep in your bed," she howled.

Mom gave in, more than likely just to shut them up. Dad frowned at her and sighed.

"Me too," whined Vanessa.

"Oh, brother," Dad groaned as they all marched into the other bedroom.

I went back to the couch and crawled under the covers.

Could Vanessa have been right? Or was Dad right when he said it was the wind? The wind was blowing pretty hard.

It couldn't have been Jamie in the girls' room. I didn't want it to be. I wanted Jamie to belong only to me.

But that bedroom must have been Jamie's at one time. Maybe Jamie didn't like the idea of Vanessa and Susan sleeping in it. Maybe he wanted it to be my room.

I closed my eyes and tried to get to sleep. I could hear creaking sounds. Some of them came from my room overhead. Old houses creaked for no reason at all, didn't they?

As my eyelids grew heavy, a soft breeze touched my forehead.

Just before I dozed off, I murmured, "Goodnight, Jamie."

7
The Library

Dad and I spent a lot of time working in the attic room. We put up paneling and painted the woodwork. It was looking great! Dad even built shelves along one wall, and I sanded and painted them.

I put the yellow rabbit inside the case with the other toys. So far, I hadn't told anyone about it. It was something I just didn't want to share. Not yet anyway. For now, it was my secret—mine and Jamie's.

———————

"Let's walk to town and check it out," Vanessa said one day.

"Good idea," I replied. "We haven't really seen it yet."

"Me too! Me too!" cried Susan, jumping up and down.

"Oh, all right," laughed Vanessa. "As though we could get away without you."

She grabbed one of Susan's hands, and I took the other.

The walk to town was only about six blocks. The first thing we came to was the school we'd be going to in a few weeks.

Mr. Hill had told Dad that all eight grades were in one school. That was because the town was so small.

I wasn't at all crazy about that. Being in the same school as my little sisters wasn't going to be fun. But a new junior high school was going to be built soon. Now that Dad's company had been built in Glenhaven, the town was expected to grow fast.

The school we would be going to was an old, two-story building. It was made of huge stones that were partly covered with climbing ivy. We stopped in front of the school and stared up at it.

"Oh, how quaint," Vanessa said, turning up her nose. "I'll bet the teachers are all at least 50 years old."

"What's wrong with it?" I asked. "I like it."

"You would."

"It looks—uh—you know—dignified."

"Right," replied Vanessa. "Dignified and dull."

It was certainly a lot different from the last school we'd gone to. Lockwood School was a flat-topped building with glass windows from ceiling to floor. It was turquoise, trimmed with gray. Not very dignified, I thought.

"I wonder which room I'll be in," said Susan.

"In the basement," Vanessa laughed and squeezed Susan's hand.

Over the wide front door of the building was written *GLENHAVEN SCHOOL 1914.*

"Hey," I said. "That's the year Jamie Harriman would have started the first grade. The same year the school was built."

"He probably went to this very school," Vanessa said. She looked me. "It will be strange, won't it? Going to the same school as a boy who lived in our house over 80 years ago?"

"Yes," I agreed. "A boy who was—" I glanced at Susan and continued quietly. "A boy who died when he was only nine years old."

"Maybe one of us will have the same teacher he did," suggested Susan.

Vanessa and I laughed.

"What's so funny?" asked Susan.

"Nothing," Vanessa and I answered, still laughing.

Vanessa grew thoughtful once more. "Jimmy, do you suppose there are any people still alive who knew Jamie Harriman? Someone who might have gone to school with him?" she asked.

"I doubt it," I replied. "They'd have to be ancient." We continued down the sidewalk.

"Poor Jamie," said Susan. "I'll bet his friends cried when they heard that he was dead."

We bought candy bars at a little grocery store on the corner, then walked to the park.

I sat on a bench eating my candy and watching Susan swing. I wondered if Jamie had played in this park. It looked old. The trees were huge. Maybe he'd had a dog, and he'd brought him here to run and play.

After we'd finished our candy, we tried out the slides and climbing bars. Then we started down Main Street.

"Some town," Vanessa said scornfully. "Not even a theater."

"But Dad said they're getting one," I reminded her. "And a shopping mall too."

Susan spoke up. "Don't forget the antique shop Mom's going to have."

"Right," I said.

"Look!" Susan was pointing at a brick building

nearly a block away. "A library," she said. "People are coming out carrying books."

"Let's go in," cried Vanessa. "I hope they have lots of good kids' books."

We walked in and found that they had shelves full of kids' books.

"All right!" Vanessa said. "There are hundreds of books here I haven't read."

I was glad that Vanessa was finding some things about the new town that she liked. She had been so upset about moving.

I wondered what she'd say if she found out the house *was* haunted. I hoped that no one else would find out.

Suddenly, I had an idea. "Come with me, Vanessa," I said. "I want to ask the librarian something."

Susan was sitting at a table with a little girl about her own age. They were turning the pages of a book together. It hadn't taken her long to make a new friend, I noticed.

I led Vanessa to the librarian's desk. Vanessa threw a questioning look at me as I spoke.

"Excuse me," I said. "Do you have old newspapers? Real old ones. Like 1917?"

The librarian smiled. "Yes, we do. Is there a special one you're interested in?"

"I'm not sure of the exact date," I answered. "It's

about the Harriman family. They used to live in the old house on Chestnut Lane."

The lady led us to a room at the back of the building. "You must be the children who moved into the Harriman house," she said. She pulled open a huge drawer and went through a stack of papers.

At last, she took a newspaper from the stack and spread it out on the table. "Such a terrible thing," she said. "I'm glad someone has bought the house. It was a shame the way it stood alone and empty for such long periods of time." She sighed. "People actually thought it was haunted."

Vanessa's mouth flew open, but before she could say anything, I blurted, "That's silly. Just because of what happened." I forced what I hoped was a laugh. "That's what my sister thinks. That the house has ghosts."

Vanessa stammered, "Well, we—we don't know if it has or not."

The librarian said, "I'm sure it hasn't." She put a hand on Vanessa's shoulder. "But when I was a child about your age, I thought there were ghosts in that old house. At least one." She took a deep breath and continued, "It was Halloween. My older brother, the two neighbor children, and I thought it would be exciting to sneak into the deserted house. My brother said it would be something to brag about at school the next day."

I saw Vanessa shiver.

"Well, we went in," said the librarian. "But we certainly didn't stay very long."

I drew close. "Why? What happened?"

"We heard something upstairs," she answered. "Like someone walking around. Of course, the house did a lot of creaking. I suppose it was from being empty for so long."

"It still creaks," said Vanessa. "And it's not empty now." She paused. "Maybe it's not creaking. Maybe it's a—"

I cut in. "It's an old house. Old houses creak. It's silly to—" I could hardly say it, "to believe in ghosts."

The woman laughed. "No one could have convinced me of that on that Halloween night. It was just as plain as anything, those footsteps. We didn't waste much time getting out of there. Later on, I decided it must have been one of my brother's pranks. Even though to this day, he swears it wasn't him."

"Then what was it?" asked Vanessa, almost in a whisper.

"I suppose our imaginations," she said. "I don't know what else it could have been." She stopped, as though her mind was going back to that night. "But—it certainly did sound like a child walking around upstairs. And another thing. As we were walking back down the road, I heard something that sounded like a child sobbing." She looked a little embarrassed as she went on. "None of the others heard it, so I guess it must have been my imagination—or maybe an owl."

Before she left the room, she said, "Let me know when you're finished."

It was several seconds before either Vanessa or I spoke. Vanessa spoke first. "I don't believe it was their imaginations, do you? How could they all imagine the same thing?"

I simply muttered, "Who knows?"

Poor Jamie. All those years in that old house. Maybe all alone. But why?

Finally, we began reading the old newspaper.

It was an eerie feeling to read about something so awful that happened in our house!

Vanessa sniffled and wiped her eyes on her shirt sleeve.

"Oh, Jimmy," she sobbed. "It's so awful. Just disappearing like that. You know they must have been—you know?"

I nodded and did a little sniffling too.

There was a picture of the Harriman family on the front page. They looked so happy. Mrs. Harriman was pretty.

The story told of the horrible findings in and around the house. The findings led the police to the conclusion that the family had been murdered.

Vanessa and I both shuddered.

"Vanessa!" I said hoarsely. "Look at this! The boy's name was James Edward! The same as mine!" Vanessa's jaw dropped.

I rubbed my eyes for a long time. At last I said, "And listen, Vanessa. The paper says that it happened on May 6, two days after Jamie's birthday. His ninth birthday."

Vanessa gulped and slumped down in her chair. "That would be May 4! Jimmy, that's your birthday too! You and Jamie have the same name *and* the same birthday!"

8
The Letter

As we walked home from town later, Susan chattered away. But Vanessa and I didn't say a word.

I could feel Vanessa's eyes on me. But when I looked up, she quickly turned her head the other way.

I didn't blame her. It was really eerie.

When we got home, I raced upstairs. I opened the case and took out the yellow rabbit. Even before I completely felt Jamie in the room, I cried, "Do you know we have the same name, Jamie? I'm James Edward too. And we have the same birthday—May 4."

The feeling of Jamie grew stronger. I wished Jamie would, or could, talk to me. There were so many things I wanted to know. I wanted to know what the school was like when it was new and Jamie was just starting the first grade. Was he scared? I had been. I'd even cried a little when Mom left. I wanted to ask Jamie if he'd had a dog. And if they'd played together in the park. I was hoping my parents would let me get a dog. I wanted to ask Jamie if he had climbed the trees in the yard and fished the lake down the road.

But most of all, I wanted Jamie to tell me what had happened. And why his spirit had stayed all these years in the old house.

The feeling that someone had been next to me was suddenly gone. But why? I was still holding the yellow rabbit.

"Jamie," I said softly.

I heard a movement behind the wall. As I listened, it got louder. There was a hinged door that Dad had built when he sealed the attic room with paneling. "We can use it for storage," he'd said.

What could be back there? Could it be a squirrel that had been closed in when Dad finished the wall?

I walked across the room and opened the small door. The sound stopped as I peered in. All I could see were some old magazines and a book. As I watched, the book moved! I was scared and wanted to run, but my feet seemed nailed to the floor. I finally reached out and picked up the book and blew the dust from it. I felt Jamie next to me once more.

"The book, Jamie?" I whispered. "What about the book?"

It was a copy of *Tom Sawyer*. Something was sticking out from between the yellowed pages. I pulled out a sealed envelope. The letter was addressed to someone named Willie Pine. Jamie's name and address were on the upper left-hand corner of the envelope. It was stamped, but it had not been mailed.

I opened it. The date at the top of the paper read *Sunday, May 6, 1917.* That was the day it had happened!

I read the letter quietly to myself.

Dear Willie,

Thank you for the birthday card. I got many nice things for my birthday. I got some lead soldiers, a book called Tom Sawyer, *and a fine baseball mitt.*

Father came home from his expedition with many interesting things. Tomorrow he will take me along when he delivers them to the museum. I will mail this letter then.

Something bad happened yesterday. Henry Fowler, the man who works for Father at the museum, came to the house. He and Father had a big argument. Father told Mr. Fowler that he would not be needing him anymore. Father says the man can't be trusted.

I look forward to your visit this summer. We will have a bully time together. We will play in my tree house and go fishing in the lake.

Your friend,
Jamie

I swallowed hard. "You wanted to tell me about the man who—"

I couldn't finish. My throat felt tight and my eyes burned.

I jumped as Mom's voice called out, "Jimmy, come down and eat." Darn!

I carefully put the letter back in the book. I put the book in the case with the rabbit and went downstairs.

Dinner was a real ordeal. I had no appetite, even though I usually liked all the things Mom had fixed. If I didn't eat, I knew she would start wondering what was wrong. I wasn't sure I could keep my secret if she started questioning me. I felt as though I was ready to explode with everything I was hiding inside.

As I nibbled at a stuffed pork chop, I thought about the letter in the book. Should I at least tell them that much? I wouldn't have to tell about Jamie. I could just say I'd found it under the rafters, which was the truth.

But there was really nothing in the letter that was important. Except the part about Henry Fowler, and everyone already knew that he was the one who had—

"Jimmy! Are you all right?" Mom was yelling.

I was choking on a piece of corn bread. Dad gave me a hard smack on the back, and the yellow lump landed on his plate.

"Really," said Mom. "You've spilled part of your milk. You have gravy on your salad. And you've dropped your fork three times."

"What's wrong with you anyway?" asked Dad.

As I mumbled, "Nothing," I heard Vanessa say, "I know."

So she *was* going to tell! I'd hoped she wouldn't. But I should have known better.

I wished she hadn't been with me at the library today. But she had been, and now she was blabbing everything. She'd tell the story the librarian had told us about that long ago Halloween. And she'd tell about Jamie and me having the same name and birthday.

Sure enough, Vanessa shared everything. Susan was the only one who spoke. "Wow!" she yelled. "Just like twins—almost!"

Mom and Dad just sat quietly. They looked at me as though I had suddenly sprouted horns or something. I jumped up from the table and ran upstairs to the attic.

9

The Lavaliere

At last, the attic room was finished. All of my belongings had been moved in.

I had fun arranging my things all by myself. I put my books and games and CD player on the shelves Dad had built. On my dresser, I put the picture of Jamie I'd found in the old desk. I placed the yellow rabbit next to the picture.

Mom had bought a new spread and throw rugs to match. When she came to see how everything looked, she spotted the yellow rabbit right away.

"Oh, Jimmy," she exclaimed. "Where in the world did this adorable little rabbit come from?"

I stammered, "I—I found it in the junk. I just thought it was kind of—uh—cute."

When Mom reached out toward the rabbit, I yelled, "Don't touch it!"

But it was too late. She already had it in her hands. "My goodness, Jimmy," she said. "What's wrong with you? I'm certainly not going to hurt it."

I swallowed. "I just didn't want things messed up. I have my room just the way I want it."

"It looks nice," she answered. "I never dreamed it could look like this when I first saw it."

She continued to hold the yellow rabbit. I held my breath—waiting—waiting.

But nothing happened. No feeling of someone else in the room. No rush of air. Nothing.

Mom went on talking. She talked about how she liked the house. About Dad's new job. About starting her own antique shop. About the nice garden we would have next summer.

Oh, please, please, I prayed under my breath. Go. Please go.

Before Mom left, she put the rabbit back on the

dresser and said, "Take good care of that rabbit, Jimmy. It's an antique. It's very valuable."

I tried to answer, but no words would come out. I only nodded and smiled at her the best I could.

The minute the door closed, I took the rabbit in my hands. I felt Jamie near me at once. So close, it felt like he was touching me.

I sat down on the bed, still holding the rabbit. The feeling of someone sitting next to me was stronger than it had ever been.

Why hadn't it happened when Mom held the yellow rabbit? Why did Jamie Harriman only come to me? Was it because we had the same name and birthday? Because of the rabbit? What was there about the rabbit? Jamie had had other toys. The lead soldiers, the top, the little boat.

"What is it, Jamie?" I blurted out. "Is there something you want me to know? Is it that you want me to take care of your rabbit for you? I will. I promise I will."

Maybe the rabbit had been given to him by someone very special. Maybe that was why I felt him in the room with me when I picked it up.

Suddenly, the rabbit became heavy. It got so heavy that I could hardly hold on to it.

All at once, it slipped from my hand and hit the floor

with a thud. A seam on the side of the cardboard rabbit opened a little.

I cried out, "Oh, no, I broke it! I broke it! I didn't mean to, Jamie. I'm so sorry."

But when I picked it up, I saw that it had not broken. There was a hinge on the side of the rabbit that I hadn't seen before. I pried it open.

I took a deep breath. My eyes widened. Inside the rabbit was a silver necklace.

The Spanish lavaliere!

"Mom! Dad!" I shouted.

I ran so fast that I almost fell down the stairs.

An hour later, we were all at the Weston Museum.

I was explaining to Mr. Farr, the man who ran the museum, how I'd found the lavaliere inside a toy rabbit. I showed him the letter too.

But I didn't tell him the rest. The part about Jamie. That was my own special secret.

"The young son must have hidden it there when the robber broke into the house," said Mr. Farr. "He tried to save it for his father." His eyes were sad. "What a brave little boy."

Mom took a hankie out of her purse and blew her nose. Vanessa and Susan were sobbing. Even Dad was sniffling a little. I wiped my eyes with the back of my hand.

"The lavaliere will be kept in the museum," said Mr. Farr. "Just the way Professor Harriman wanted."

———————

I could hardly wait to get upstairs to my room when we got back home.

I took the yellow rabbit in my hand and sat down on the bed.

"Everything is okay now, Jamie," I said. "The lavaliere is safe in the museum. That's what you wanted, wasn't it? That's what you were trying to let me know?"

But something was wrong. There was no feeling of Jamie in the room.

I was alone.

"Jamie!" I called out. "Come back! Please come back!"

But deep inside, I knew that Jamie had to leave. He was at rest now. He was where he belonged.

I was sad. I'd miss Jamie a lot. But I'd always remember him. Every time I looked at the yellow rabbit.